WHY THE TIDES
EBB AND FLOW

Joan Chase Bowden

Illustrated by Marc Brown

Houghton Mifflin Company   Boston

Library of Congress Cataloging-in-Publication Data

Bowden, Joan Chase.
  Why the tides ebb and flow.
  Summary: In this folktale explaining why the sea has tides, an old woman threatens
to pull the rock from the hole in the ocean floor if Sky Spirit does not honor his promise
to give her shelter.
  ISBN 0-395-28378-7
  [1. Folklore]   I. Brown, Marc Tolon.   II. Title.
PZ8.1.B665Wh   79-12359
398.2'6
[E]

Printed in the United States of America

RNF ISBN 0-395-28378-7
PAP ISBN 0-395-54952-3

WOZ 10 9 8 7 6 5

To Sandy, Andrew, and Pamela Jane
and to
all their brothers and sisters
everywhere

Not in my time, not in your time, but in the old time, when the earth and sea were new, a stubborn old woman had no hut. She lived all by herself in the middle of a flower patch.

When the winds blew, she was cold. When the rains came, she was wet. And when the sun shone down, she was neither cold nor wet, but she was burned from top to toe.

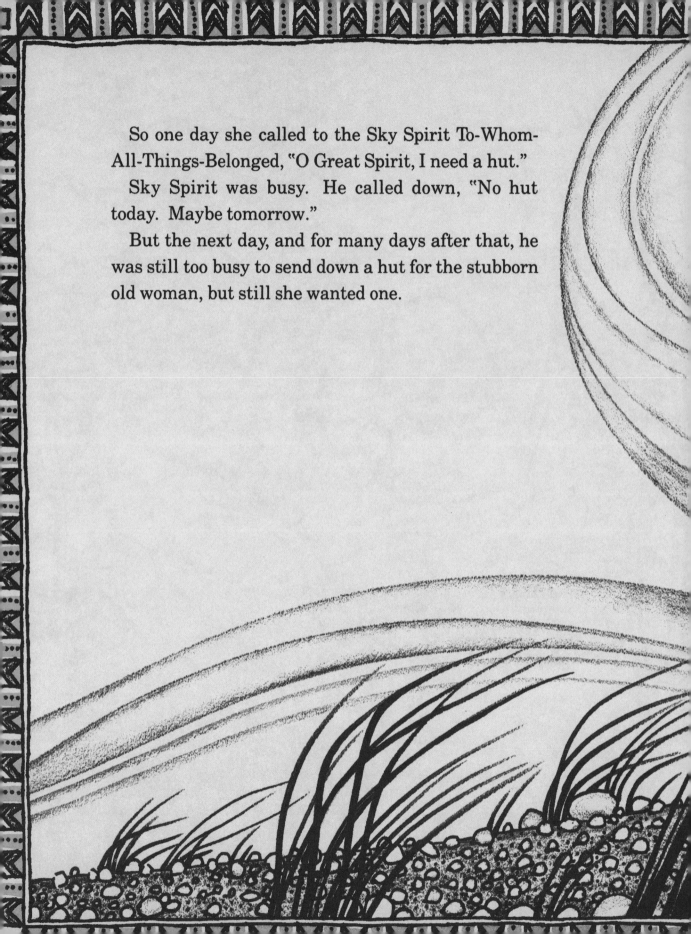

So one day she called to the Sky Spirit To-Whom-All-Things-Belonged, "O Great Spirit, I need a hut."

Sky Spirit was busy. He called down, "No hut today. Maybe tomorrow."

But the next day, and for many days after that, he was still too busy to send down a hut for the stubborn old woman, but still she wanted one.

So another day, after thinking and thinking, Old Woman called, "Then give me a rock to shelter me from the weather."

Sky Spirit was too busy to have been thinking and thinking. Too quickly, he answered, "Take one."

Then how happy was the stubborn old woman.

She knew exactly which rock she wanted. So she climbed into her stewpot and set sail on the great green ocean.

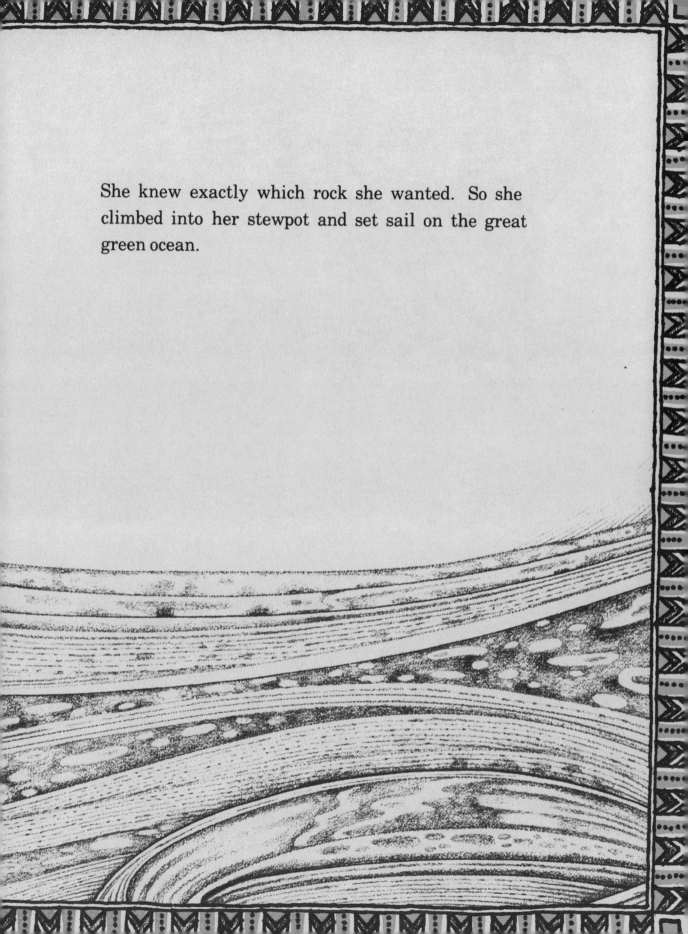

She sailed along, and she sailed along, and soon she saw Sea Bird.

He called:

> "Ai-ee, Old Woman,
> Listen to me.
> You are sailing too close
> To the hole in the sea."

"Oho!" answered Old Woman, "then I think I am sailing in the right direction."

She sailed along, and she sailed along, and soon she saw Little Silver Fish.

He called:

> "Ai-oo, Old Woman,
> Listen to me!
> You are much, much too close
> To the hole in the sea."

"Aha!" answered Old Woman, "then I *know* I am sailing in the right direction."

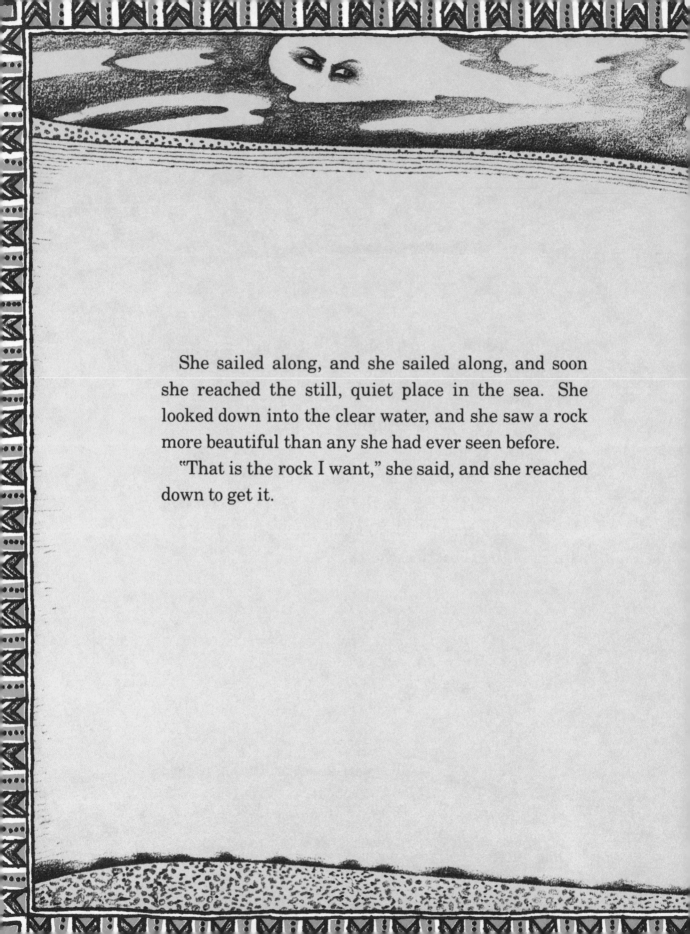

She sailed along, and she sailed along, and soon she reached the still, quiet place in the sea. She looked down into the clear water, and she saw a rock more beautiful than any she had ever seen before.

"That is the rock I want," she said, and she reached down to get it.

But at that very moment, busy Sky Spirit called to
her from his hut in the clouds:

"Old Woman, Old Woman,

Listen to me!

DON'T take the rock

From the hole in the sea!"

Stubborn Old Woman answered, "But that's the
rock I want!" And she reached down and down.

Then Sky Spirit called again:
"Old Woman, Old Woman,
Are you listening to me?
I think you are taking
The rock from the sea."

Stubborn Old Woman answered, "But that's the rock I need!" And she reached down and down.

Then Sky Spirit called for a third time:
"Old Woman, Old Woman,
You're NOT listening to me.
Be SURE you don't take
The rock from the sea!"

Stubborn Old Woman answered, "BUT YOU SAID I COULD HAVE IT!"

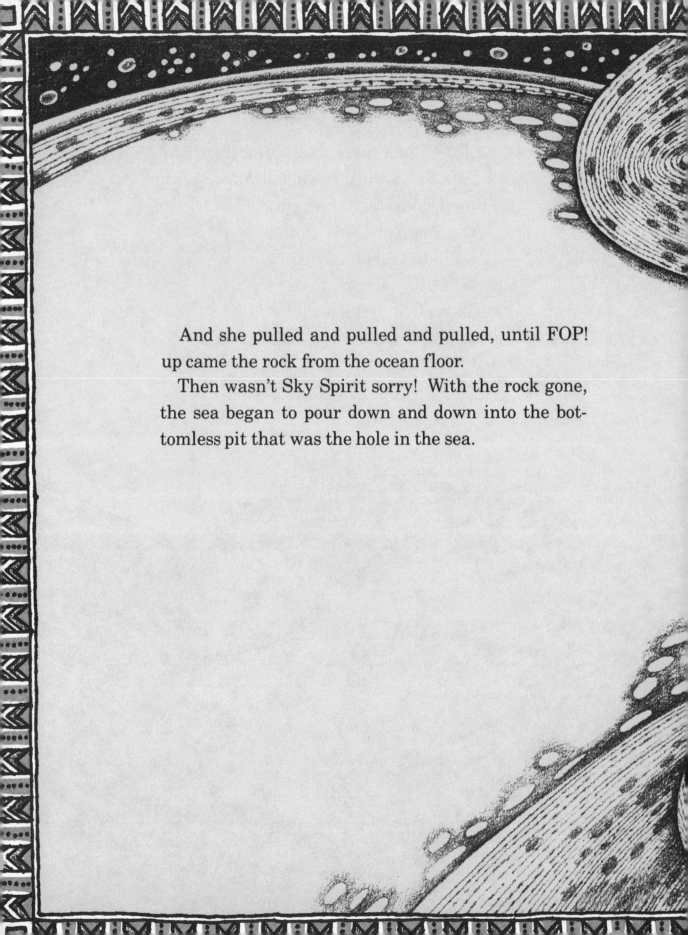

And she pulled and pulled and pulled, until FOP!
up came the rock from the ocean floor.

Then wasn't Sky Spirit sorry! With the rock gone,
the sea began to pour down and down into the bot-
tomless pit that was the hole in the sea.

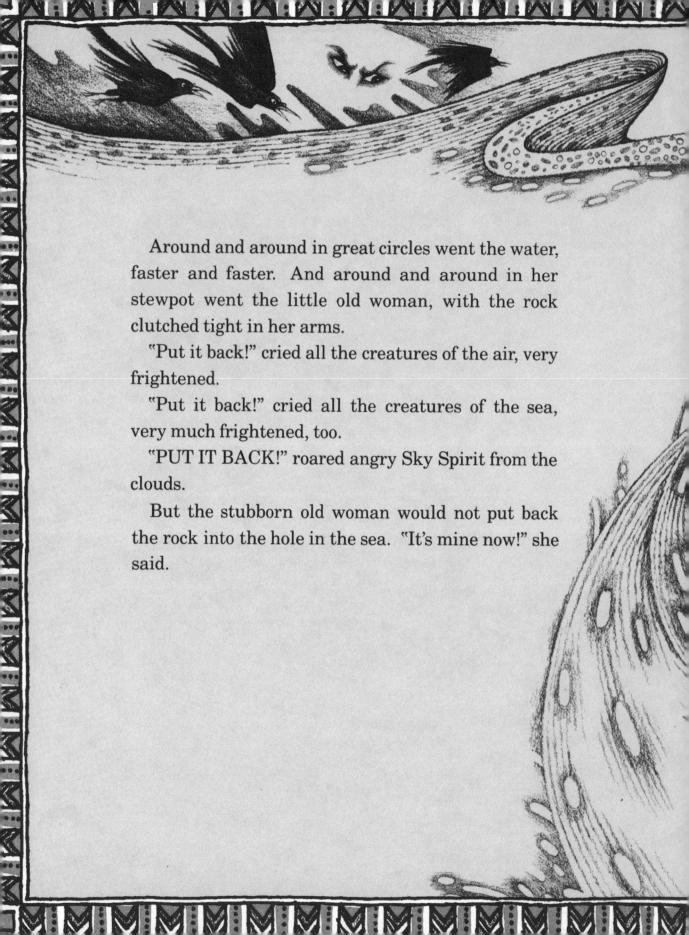

Around and around in great circles went the water, faster and faster. And around and around in her stewpot went the little old woman, with the rock clutched tight in her arms.

"Put it back!" cried all the creatures of the air, very frightened.

"Put it back!" cried all the creatures of the sea, very much frightened, too.

"PUT IT BACK!" roared angry Sky Spirit from the clouds.

But the stubborn old woman would not put back the rock into the hole in the sea. "It's mine now!" she said.

So Sky Spirit had to hurry and send Little Dog down to earth.

"Go put your nose in the hole in the sea!" commanded Sky Spirit. And Little Dog did.

But his nose was too small, and the water was too cold, and down, down went the sea, *m'tia, m'toa,* TLOP!

Then Old Woman took shivering Little Dog into her stewpot. "From now on, you can be my little dog," she said, "and I will love you always."

Then Sky Spirit had to hurry and send Young Maiden down to earth.

"Go kneel in the hole in the sea!" he commanded. And Young Maiden did.

But her knees were too small, and the water was too cold. And down, down went the sea, *m'tia, m'toa,* TLOP!

Old Woman took shivering Young Maiden into her stewpot, too. "From now on, you will be my daughter," she said, "and I will love you forever."

For one last time, Sky Spirit had to hurry. He sent strong Young Man down to earth.

"Go sit in the hole in the sea!" commanded Sky Spirit. And strong Young Man did.

But still the hole was too big, and the water too cold. And down, down went the sea as before, *m'tia, m'toa*, TLOP!

Then Old Woman also took shivering Young Man
into her stewpot. "From now on, you will be my
daughter's husband," she said, "and I will love you,
too."

They all clung together in the stewpot as it spun around and around in ever smaller circles, closer and closer to the hole in the sea.

"Put back the rock!" cried all the creatures of the sea.

"Put back the rock!" cried all the creatures of the air.

"Put back the rock," cried Sky Spirit, "and I will let you borrow it twice each day forevermore to pretty up your flower patch."

The stubborn old woman looked at Little Dog, who would love and protect her. She looked at Young Maiden, who would keep her company when the long day's work was done.

She looked at strong Young Man, *who would build her a hut!*
And Old Woman smiled.

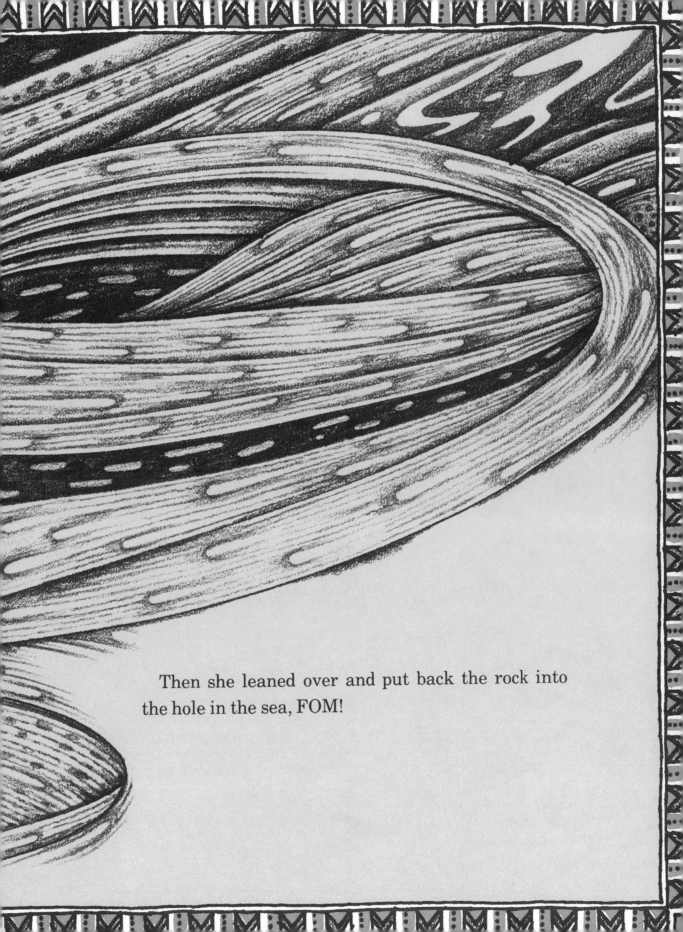

Then she leaned over and put back the rock into the hole in the sea, FOM!

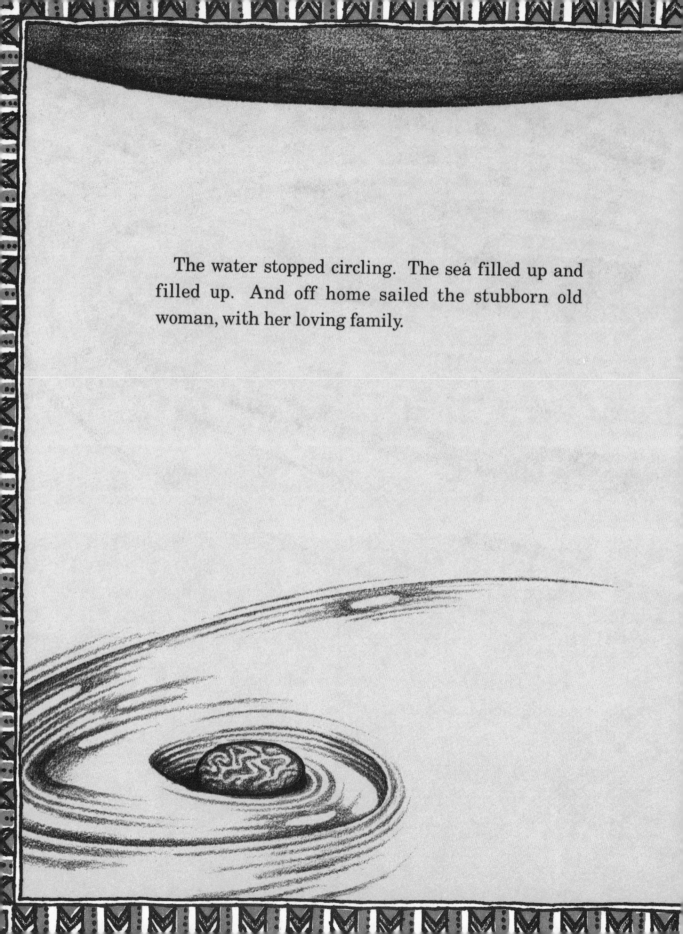

The water stopped circling. The sea filled up and filled up. And off home sailed the stubborn old woman, with her loving family.

But twice each day, she still goes a-sailing in her stewpot. Twice each day, she borrows the rock to pretty up her flower patch.

As she takes the rock away, the water goes down and down into the hole in the sea. That is low tide.

As she puts the rock back, the sea fills up and fills up. That is high tide. To this day, that is why the tides ebb and flow.

But some parts of Little Dog, Young Maiden, and Young Man never did warm up.

To this day, that is why all Little Dog's children have cold noses. That is why all Young Maiden's daughters have cold knees. And to this day, that is why all Young Man's sons stand with their backs to the fire.